Jen the Hen

J...nd ...ins

HARCOURT BRACE & COMPANY
Orlando   Atlanta   Austin   Boston   San Francisco   Chicago   Dallas   New York
Toronto   London

Have you heard of
Jen the hen?

h

One day she went to her den.

d

Jen looked in her bag for paper and pen.

p

Then she wrote a letter to Ken and Ben, the garden men.

m

Jen signed it and stamped it, and gave it to Wren.

Wren flew over the glen looking for Ken and Ben.

B

Ken and Ben
The Garden Men.

She landed on Ben and gave the letter to Ken.

The letter from Jen said to meet her at ten.

t

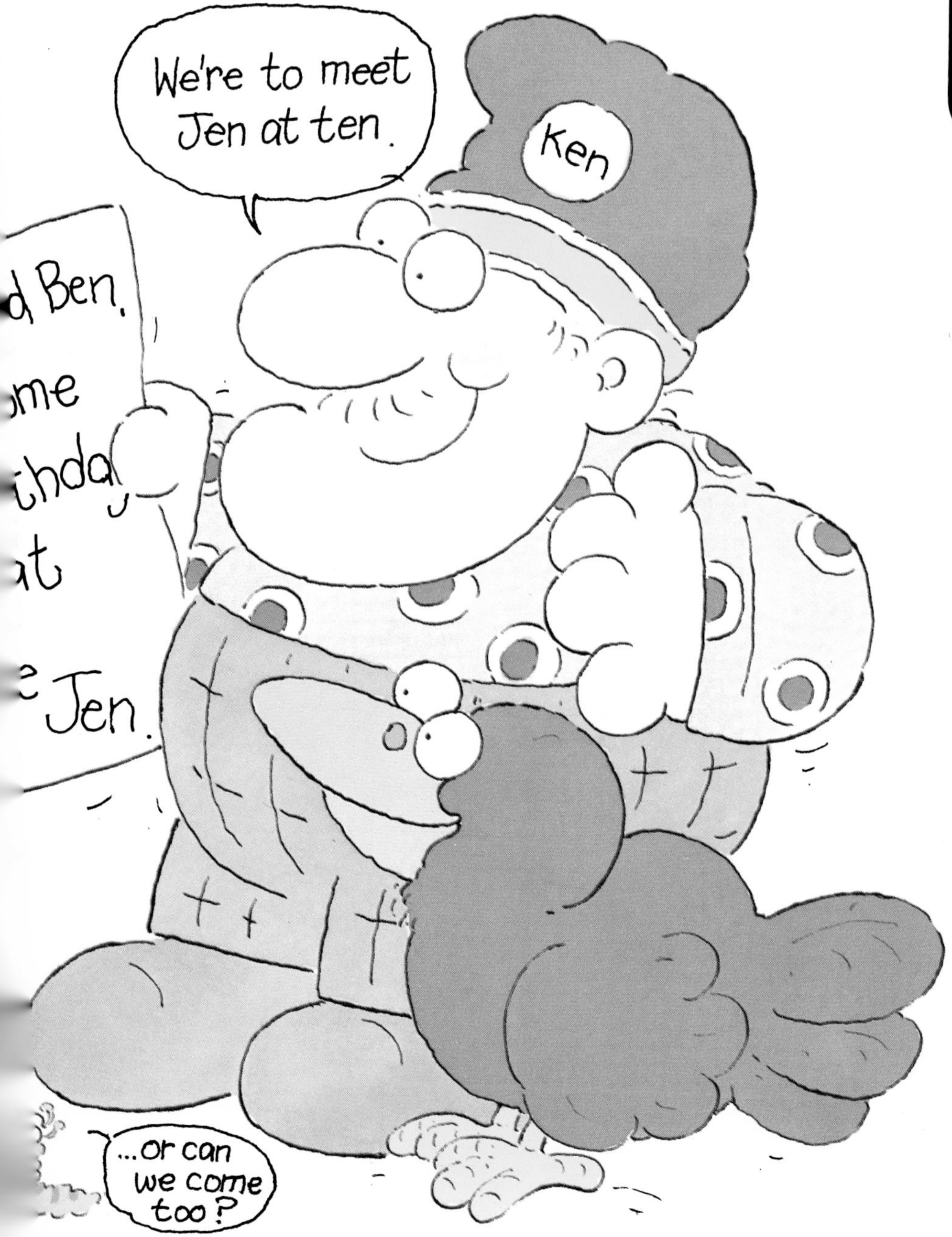

Exactly at ten, they all met in the glen — Ken, Ben and Wren — and a hen called Jen.

Jen

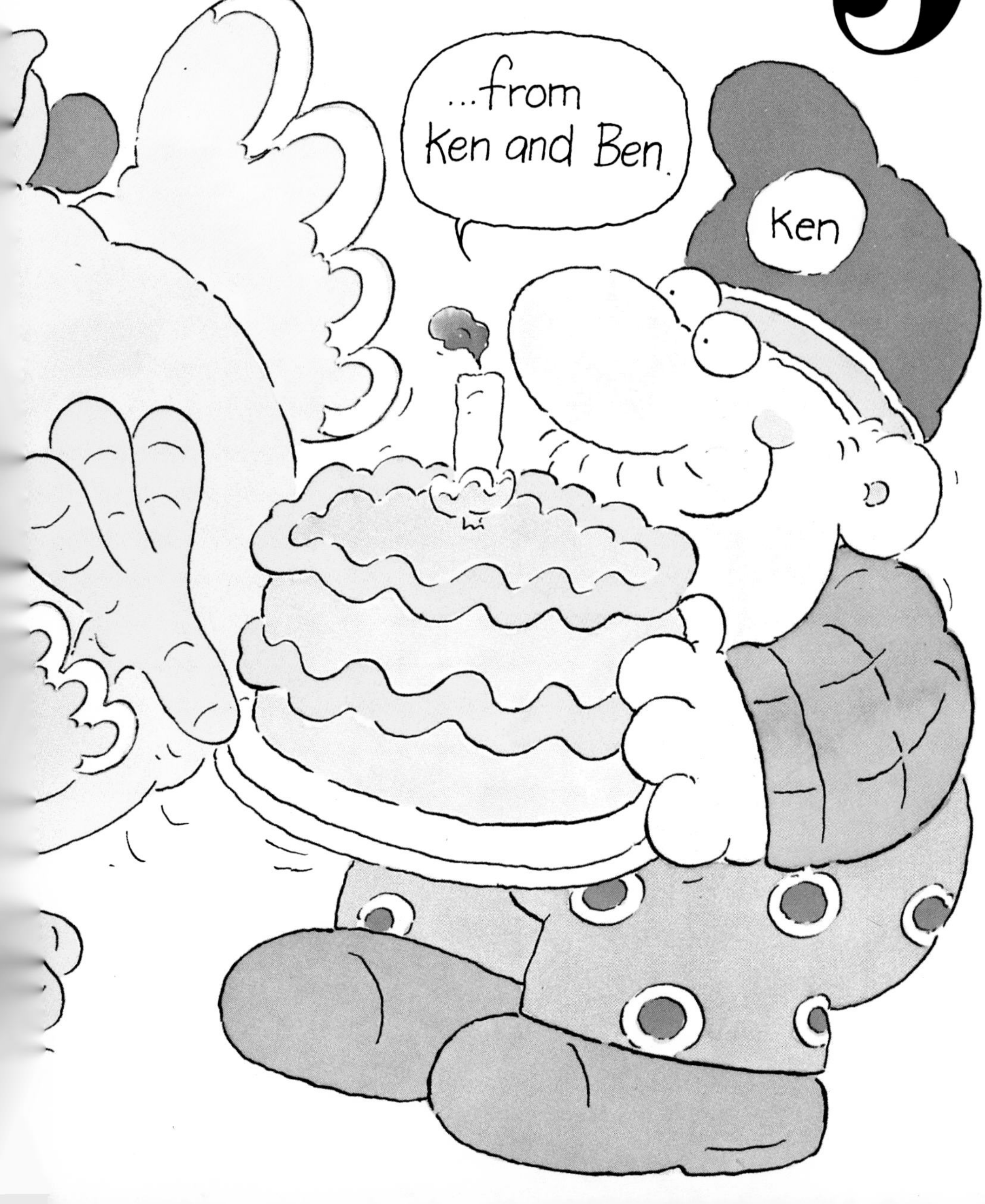

This edition is published by special arrangement with G. P. Putnam's Sons, a division of The Putnam & Grosset Group.

Grateful acknowledgment is made to G. P. Putnam's Sons, a division of The Putnam Publishing Group for permission to reprint *Jen the Hen* by Colin and Jacqui Hawkins. Copyright © 1985 by Colin and Jacqui Hawkins.

Printed in the United States of America

ISBN 0-15-300311-1

5 6 7 8 9 10   059   96   95   94